Beast Quest®

Stealth
THE
GHOST PANTHER

BY ADAM BLADE

ORCHARD

THE FORBIDDEN LAND

THE DEAD VALLEY

THE DEAD JUNGLE

THE DARK WOOD

THE DEAD PEAKS

CONTENTS

All hail, fellow followers of the Quest.

We have not met before, but like you, I have been watching Tom's adventures with a close eye. Do you know who I am? Have you heard of Taladon the Swift, Master of the Beasts? I have returned – just in time for my son, Tom, to save me from a fate worse than death. The Dark Wizard, Malvel, has stolen something precious from me, and until Tom is able to complete another Quest, I must wait between worlds, neither human nor ghost. I am half the man I once was and only Tom can return me to my former glory.

Will Tom have the strength of heart to help his father? This new Quest would test even the most determined hero. And there may be a heavy price for my son to pay if he defeats six more Beasts…

All I can do is hope – that Tom is successful and that I will one day be restored to full strength. Will you put your power behind Tom and wish him well? I know I can count on my son – can I count on you, too? Not a moment can be wasted. As this latest Quest unfolds, much rides upon it.

We must all be brave.

Taladon

PROLOGUE

Luke peered cautiously around the
street corner. Nothing moved, except
for a cat that shot across the cobbles
and vanished between two buildings
on the opposite side. All the dwellers
in the main city of Avantia had gone
to their beds long ago.

The moon shed a pale light over the
street, though dark shadows lurked
in corners. Beyond the rooftops of the

shops and houses, Luke could see the purple spires of King Hugo's palace. He shivered as he wondered if Wizard Aduro was looking out, keeping watch over everything that went on in the city.

A hand shoved Luke roughly in the back; he glanced over his shoulder to see his master, Bill.

"What are you waiting for?" Bill demanded. "Get a move on!"

"Just checking," Luke mumbled resentfully.

He looked up at the creaking inn sign above his head, it showed a scarlet dragon with fire spurting from its jaws. Bill pointed to a pile of barrels stacked against the inn wall. "Go on. Climb," he ordered.

Luke hung back. The climb was easy enough – above the pile of barrels a drainpipe led up to an open latticed window. But he was scared at the thought of what would happen if anyone found him once he was inside.

"I said, climb!" Bill gave Luke a harder shove that sent him stumbling to his knees. "You're a young lad, it's easy for you to scramble up there. Get inside, and come down to let me in." He chuckled and rubbed his grimy hands together. "There'll be rich pickings tonight, and you'll get your share."

Luke hauled himself to his feet and limped towards the pile of barrels.

He didn't dare disobey Bill. His master was a huge man, tall and

broad-shouldered, and he could scare
Luke just by glaring at him.

I never wanted to be a thief, Luke
thought miserably as he started to

clamber up the drainpipe. *How did I end up like this?*

As he climbed, he thought he could hear soft footsteps in the street, and a sound like a whip cracking in the air. Then he heard the scuffle of Bill's boots on the cobbles, and his master's voice raised in a shout that died away at once in a choking rattle.

Luke peered over his shoulder. Bill was lying face down in the street.

A pool of blood spread slowly from his temple, glistening ink-black in the light of the moon.

Is he dead? Terror froze Luke to the drainpipe.

A moment later, Bill stirred, hauled himself to his knees and then to his feet.

"What happened?" Luke called down softly. "Are you all right?"

Bill didn't reply. Staggering forwards, he pointed a trembling finger at Luke. "Thief!" he spat, his eyes narrowed. "I'm going to tell your parents what you've been up to!"

Luke gasped in horror. His mother and father would never live down the shame of knowing that he crept out of bed at night to go thieving with Bill. And Bill might have been rough with him before, but never cruel. What had happened to him?

"You can't—" he began.

His protest was cut off by a blood-curdling howl that echoed through the streets of the city. It sounded like the yowl of a hunting cat, but a thousand times louder and more menacing. Bill started at the sound, then turned and raced away.

Luke could see nothing in the empty street except a pair of glittering yellow dots, dancing in the distance.

"What's that?" he muttered to himself. "They look like eyes."

Cautiously he began to climb down, only to freeze as the green dots suddenly leapt forwards. Out of the night a coal-black panther appeared, its gleaming fangs bared and its jaws gaping as if it might swallow Luke whole.

With a choking cry, Luke scrambled back up the drainpipe. *Is that what attacked Bill?* he asked himself as he tried to grip the slippery surface.

The panther leapt and snarled below him. Sword-like claws slashed beneath Luke's feet. Its teeth were veined like marble, and three tails whipped through the air behind it. Around its neck was a thick leather collar from which dangled an odd-shaped piece of gold.

As Luke watched, a rat scurried out from behind the pile of barrels. He gasped in amazement as the Beast lashed out with one of its tails, lassoing the squealing rat around the middle, before tossing the vermin into its open mouth.

Swallowing the creature in one gulp, the Beast turned back to gaze up at Luke. Its amber eyes burned

through the darkness. Luke told his body to move, to keep on clambering up the drainpipe, but he couldn't make his arms and legs obey. His gaze was locked with the Beast's as the panther began to circle one of its three tails. The tail moved faster and faster until it snaked out through the air and snatched Luke's ankle.

Luke kicked out, but he couldn't break the grip of the Beast's tail. His hands scrabbled uselessly at the wall of the inn as he felt himself being dragged down.

It's going to eat me, he thought frantically, letting out a shriek of terror. *It'll swallow me up, just like it did that rat...*

EVIL IN THE CITY

Tom stood beside Elenna on the edge of the volcano at Stonewin and looked down at the piece of amulet that he held in the palm of his hand. The gold shone in the sunlight and the piece of enamel glowed and winked like a blue eye.

"That's five pieces," he said. "Only one more to go."

Pulling on the leather thong around

his neck, he fished the rest of the amulet out from under his tunic and fitted the new piece into place. Golden light flared briefly. When it died away the new piece had joined with the rest as if it had never been broken off. A jagged gap showed where the final piece was still missing.

"It won't be long now," Elenna said. "Then your father will be fully returned to his old self."

Tom nodded slowly. "But I've lost another of my special powers," he reminded his friend. "I haven't got the strength of heart from the golden chainmail anymore. And that helped me through so many of our Quests."

"You don't need it!" Elenna assured him. "You've got enough courage of your own."

Storm, Tom's black stallion, blew out a noisy breath as if he was agreeing, and Elenna's grey wolf, Silver, gave a long howl.

"See?" Elenna went on. "They know you're brave enough for anything! And so does your father."

Tom smiled at her, feeling a wave of determination fill his chest. His father, Taladon, had been captured by Malvel, the Dark Wizard. Although he had escaped when Tom defeated Malvel for the third time, he was trapped as a ghost between the real world and the spirit world. Taladon could only return to life when the six pieces of the Amulet of Avantia had been joined together. But Malvel had

given the pieces to six Ghost Beasts.
Tom had already defeated five of
the powerful monsters, but he still
had to face the sixth. And he knew
that this last Beast would be the
deadliest of all.

"So where do we go next?" Elenna
asked.

Tom stretched out one hand.
"Map!" he commanded.

The ghostly map given to them by
Wizard Aduro took shape in front of
him, bobbing gently in the air.

A shimmering path appeared,
leading from the volcano to the main
city of Avantia.

"That's where King Hugo's palace
is!" Elenna exclaimed. "Surely the
Ghost Beast wouldn't dare go there?"

"I don't know." A cold sense of approaching evil crept through Tom. "Maybe that's what my father meant when he said the next Beast would be closer to home."

"And more evil than we can possibly know," Elenna added. "It must be really cunning to have hidden itself in the very heart of Avantia – let alone to go near King Hugo and Wizard Aduro."

Tom felt his hands ball into fists.

"I don't care how cunning it is. We'll defeat it!"

Beside the picture of the city a small black shape came into view: a panther with a coat the colour of night. It snarled at Tom as he gazed at it, and slid out gleaming claws.

At the same moment a chilly wind
blew past Tom, bringing the foul
stench of something rotten. The voice
of evil Wizard Malvel whispered in
Tom's ear. "Stealth..."

"Stealth!" Elenna exclaimed; clearly
she had heard the whisper too. She
exchanged a startled glance with Tom.
"Is that the name of the Ghost Beast?"

"It must be," Tom declared. "And we
were right. The Beast *is* in the city."

"And that means it's not just our own safety we have to worry about," Elenna said. "The king and everyone else are in danger too."

Tom's stomach churned with a mixture of fear and excitement. "We'd better get moving," he said. "This Beast could destroy the whole of Avantia."

Digging into his pocket, Tom drew out the compass that his father had given to him. There were two points on it: *Destiny* and *Danger*. He held it out towards the city and watched as the needle swung round to *Destiny*.

"That proves it. There's no time to waste," he said, closing up the compass and stowing it away again. "What's the quickest way of getting to the city?"

"The piece of Tagus's horseshoe will

give us extra speed," Elenna said, pointing to the horse-man's gift, which was fixed onto Tom's shield.

"Yes, but we need to choose the quickest route."

Tom studied the map again, but it only showed the main road that wound through the hills and fields of Avantia, taking in many towns and villages on its way. He banished the map with a flick of his fingers, and looked around thoughtfully. Then his gaze fell on the mouth of one of the tunnels at the base of the volcano.

"Look!" he cried excitedly, gesturing towards it. "Remember how we rescued the people of Stonewin from the fires of Epos, back on our first Quest?"

"We led them through the tunnels,"

Elenna replied, her eyes shining as she understood Tom's plan. "They go all the way to the city."

"Yes." A wide grin split Tom's face. "And we can use those tunnels again!"

2

HELP FROM THE VILLAGE

Tom set off at a run, speeding along the path that wound down the side of the volcano. *I don't need the golden leg armour any more,* he thought. Running downhill, *I can go as fast as I dare!*

Storm cantered ahead, his hooves throwing up spurts of black volcanic dust, while Elenna and Silver raced alongside each other, hard on Tom's heels. Tom loved the feeling of the wind as it whipped his hair back from his face. *This would be fun,* he said to himself, *if we weren't on such a serious Quest.*

Tom slowed his pace to a jog as they reached the foot of the volcano and headed through the woods. Now he took the lead, weaving his way through the trees towards the tunnels.

At last Tom and his friends halted, panting, by the biggest tunnel mouth. Inside, Tom could see a passageway leading into blackness.

"It's dark," Tom began. "How are we going to—"

He was interrupted by a shout

coming from the direction of the
village. "Greetings!"

Tom turned to see a group of
villagers hurrying towards them.

In the lead was Raymond, who had helped guide his people to safety when the volcano was about to erupt. Just behind him was a young boy, Owen, and his mother, Nesta. Owen was still fair-haired and skinny, but much taller than when Tom and Elenna had last seen him.

"It's Tom and Elenna!" Raymond exclaimed, throwing his arms around Tom. "What are you doing in these parts?"

"I hope there's no more trouble with Epos," Nesta said as she embraced Elenna.

"No, Epos protects the kingdom now," Tom replied quietly, remembering how the magnificent flame bird had helped him and

Elenna in their Quest against Blaze the Ice Dragon. He clapped Owen on the shoulder. "It's good to see you again!"

But even as he spoke, Tom thought that the villagers didn't seem quite as friendly as he remembered them. He had felt a shiver pass through him as Raymond hugged him. Somehow Owen's mischievous face seemed to have turned cold, and there was a dark glint in Nesta's eyes as she released Elenna. Her sleeves were rolled up, as if she had been working in the kitchen, and there was a long red scratch down one of her arms.

Nesta laughed as she spotted Tom looking at the scratch. "It's nothing!" she assured him, hurriedly rolling her sleeves down. "I got it picking gooseberries. Those thorns!"

"You're welcome to stay with us," Raymond invited them. "We'll never forget what you did for Stonewin."

"Thank you, but we can't stay," Tom replied. He didn't want to share all the details of their Quest, in case word of the Ghost Beasts sent the villagers into a panic. "We have to get back to The City as quickly as we can, so we thought we would go through the tunnels."

"Do you have any candles we could use?" Elenna asked.

"We can do better than that," Raymond told her. "If you come back to the village with us, we'll give you some lamps."

Tom and Elenna exchanged a glance.

"Time's slipping away," Tom muttered into his friend's ear. "We ought to set out as soon as we can."

"We don't seem to have much choice," Elenna replied. She pointed to where Owen and the other village children were already clustered around Silver, patting him and running their hands through his thick fur, while one of the adult villagers had taken Storm by the bridle and was leading him away. "Besides, if we don't go to the village, we'll have to make torches somehow."

Tom nodded. "And that might take longer than fetching the lamps." He turned to Raymond. "Thanks.

We'll come with you, but only to pick up the lamps. It's already late and we really need to be on our way."

"Of course!" Raymond smiled as he glanced round at the other villagers. "We'll do everything we can to help."

Another shiver passed through Tom as he saw the jubilant looks some of the villagers were sharing. *Could they really be that happy we're coming to visit?*

Raymond led the way along a path that wound through the woods and joined the main street of the village. At the far end was a sturdy hut built of logs. Through the window, Tom could see shelves full of supplies. There were boxes of candles and a row of lamps hanging from the roof.

Raymond flung open the door. "Go in," he said, gesturing to Tom and Elenna. "Take whatever you want."

Tom stepped inside the store, followed by Elenna. He still felt uneasy, he wanted to find what they needed, and get out of the village as quickly as they could.

He took several boxes of candles from one of the shelves, shoving them into his pockets, while Elenna lifted two of the lamps down from their hooks and carefully filled them with oil from an earthenware jar.

"That should be enough—" Tom began, breaking off at a sharp bang behind him. When he spun round he saw that the door had slammed shut.

Tom's uneasiness flared into alarm.

He ran across to the door and tugged on the handle. But the door wouldn't move.

"It's locked!" Tom exclaimed.

3

MALVEL'S PLOT

Tom and Elenna ran to the window, but it was too small to climb through. Outside, the villagers were crowding around, laughing. Nesta rolled up her sleeve and waved her scarred arm in front of Tom and Elenna.

"Gooseberries!" she cried. "Were you really such fools as to believe that? The three-tailed Beast gave me this wound, and I'm proud of it!"

"You won't defeat *this* Beast!" Owen added, rolling up his own sleeve to show a long scratch from elbow to wrist.

Tom glanced at Elenna. Her eyes were wide with alarm. *"Three* tails?" she whispered. "What Beast are they talking about?"

Around Nesta, Raymond and the other villagers were showing off their own scratches from the Beast.

"That's what was wrong!" Tom exclaimed, punching at the windowsill in frustration. "I knew there was something. The whole village has been changed!"

One by one the villagers began to move off, turning their backs and leaving Tom and Elenna in their prison. A man grabbed Storm's bridle and tried to lead him away. The black stallion reared up, his fore-hooves striking the air as he let out a furious neigh. Silver darted forwards, nipping at the man's heels. With a roar of rage he let go of the bridle. Storm turned and fled down the street in a thunder of hooves, with Silver racing alongside, back towards the tunnels.

"Silver! Silver!" Elenna cried out.

"It's all right," said Tom, putting a hand on her shoulder. "They'll wait for us in the woods. They'd never leave us, but they have more sense than to stay with these evil villagers."

Elenna nodded, though she still looked upset. "At least we don't have to worry about them," she said.

"We need to find out what's going on," Tom decided. "I still have one last power from the Golden Armour. I can use my magical sight from the golden helmet to look for clues."

He dragged a wooden box over to the window and scrambled up on it to give himself the best possible view. *The Beast must have left some traces when it visited the village,* he told himself, as he peered down the street. *There might be something to help me track it down.*

He let his magical gaze travel down the street, examining the shops and houses.

"What can you see?" Elenna asked anxiously.

"Nothing," Tom replied. "I don't think – no, wait! What's that?"

He fixed his gaze on a spot beyond the last houses of the village, where the cobbled street gave way to a path of beaten earth. In the earth were huge pawprints, leading back towards the tunnels.

Tom felt the blood drain from his face as he turned to Elenna. "Pawprints," he murmured hoarsely. "Huge, like a massive cat's."

Elenna frowned. "I don't understand."

"I'm afraid I do." Tom jumped down from the box and stood next to her, pointing out of the window. Inwardly he cursed himself for not piecing the evidence together sooner. "The villagers of Stonewin would never usually behave like this. Nesta said that a Beast with three tails made the claw-mark on her arm. And all the others have claw-marks, too."

"And there are giant pawprints on the ground!" Elenna exclaimed, suddenly grasping what Tom meant.

"Yes. The Beast that made the marks is the last Ghost Beast. Stealth has attacked the village!"

Elenna nodded slowly. "So that's his evil magic – to turn good people bad!"

Tom looked out of the window again, up to the slopes of the volcano. "Do you remember what Malvel said after we defeated Blaze the Ice Dragon? He said, 'another time'."

Elenna clenched her fists. "The Dark Wizard isn't going to give up."

Tom nodded in agreement, feeling sick with worry for his friends in The City, and for the family he had left behind in Errinel. "Malvel is inflicting the worst injury he possibly could on Avantia. He's trying to turn everyone evil!"

"We've got to get out of here," Elenna said.

"And there's no time to waste." Tom strode back to the door and wrenched at the handle again. "Stealth is in The City. What if he has already turned King Hugo and Wizard Aduro evil?"

The lock wouldn't give way to Tom's desperate tugging. Elenna took an arrow out of her quiver and pulled the head off the shaft.

"Maybe I can force the lock," she said as she poked the arrow-point into the keyhole.

Tom watched her for a moment, but she wasn't having any success. The arrowhead was too big to get far enough inside the lock, and the point kept slipping out.

Forcing back panic, Tom began grabbing things from the shelves, tossing aside rolls of linen, jars

of nails and bags of wheat as he searched for something that would help him force the door. Looking at all the useless supplies, his frustration boiled over.

"There's nothing here that will help!"

Elenna straightened up, brushing a lock of hair out of her eyes. "It's no good," she announced.

Tom glanced around frantically. Fear tingled in his belly. He forced himself to take a deep breath. He had to stay calm. *There must be some way out of here,* he told himself. *And I'm going to find it!*

1

ESCAPE!

Tom noticed a big iron hook fixed to the central roof-beam of the store.

He guessed it was meant for hauling heavy items up onto high shelves. He pictured a rope slung over it, raising a load...

"Yes!" he exclaimed. "That's it!"

He scrabbled among the scattered supplies until he found a coil of thick rope. Unrolling it, he flung one end over the hook, and handed the other to Elenna. "Hold that taut, and brace yourself," he instructed her.

With Elenna gripping the rope, Tom swarmed up it. But as he gazed upwards, he spotted the strands fraying where they were looped over the metal hook.

"I'm coming down!" he called to Elenna. "The rope's going to break."

He began climbing rapidly down again, but before his feet touched the floor, the rope gave way. With a cry of alarm, Tom hurtled to the ground, jarring his shoulder as he hit the floorboards.

Elenna dropped the rope and knelt beside Tom. "Are you hurt?" she asked anxiously.

Tom sat up, wincing with pain as he massaged his shoulder. "It's nothing much," he said. "Pass me my shield, please."

When Elenna had brought the shield, Tom took the talon he had received from Epos the Flame Bird out of its slot, and pressed it to his shoulder. At once the pain died away and a cool sensation spread over it. Letting out a sigh of relief, Tom moved his arm up and down to check that the damage was really healed.

"It's fine now," he told Elenna, who was looking on anxiously. "Epos's talon works really well!"

Tom slotted the talon carefully back into his shield and sprang to his feet. He may not be hurt any more, but they were no nearer to getting out of their prison. "Now what do we do?" he murmured, half to himself. "I'm not trusting that rope again."

"I know!" Elenna exclaimed. She swooped down on one of the rolls of linen Tom had tossed aside while he was searching, and began to tear strips off it. Then she knotted them together to make a rope. As soon as he realised what Elenna meant to do, Tom knelt beside her and tested the knots, pulling them as tight as he could.

"It's not perfect," Elenna said, "but it's better than nothing."

"Better than the rope, anyway," Tom agreed.

As soon as the knotted linen was

long enough, Tom tossed it over the
hook. With Elenna holding the other
end, he leapt into the air and swung
himself in an arc towards the door.
He held his feet braced in front of
him, ready for the impact.

As Tom hit the door it started to
give way, but the strong wooden
planks remained in place.

"Try again!" Elenna cried excitedly.

Tom leapt up and swung himself at the door once more. This time, when his feet slammed into it, the door burst open. Tom smashed through, into the open, scattering splinters of wood everywhere. Triumph surging through him, he landed with a thud, staggered, and regained his balance.

"Come on!" he urged, glancing back at Elenna. "The whole village must have heard that."

Elenna grabbed Tom's shield and thrust it into his hands as she darted out to join him. At the same moment, Tom heard an angry shout from further down the street. A crowd of men surged out of the inn.

Raymond was in the lead. He spotted Tom and Elenna. "They're escaping!" he shouted.

The whole crowd pounded down the street towards the store hut. Determination coursed through Tom. He *wouldn't* let these evil villagers put him and his friend in prison again.

"Let's go!" he yelled.

5

THROUGH THE TUNNELS

"What about the candles?" Elenna gasped as they began running as fast as they could down the street.

"In my pockets," Tom replied. "Come on!"

The villagers were hard on their heels. Tom cast a rapid glance over his shoulder. Raymond was at the head of the crowd, waving his fists.

His flapping shirt sleeves showed the marks of Stealth's claws on his arms.

"Faster!" Tom panted. "They're gaining!"

As he and Elenna turned off the village street and pelted down the path that led to the tunnels, Tom heard the beat of a horse's hooves and the drawn-out howl of a wolf. Storm came cantering out of the trees, with Silver bounding along beside him.

"I knew they wouldn't leave us!" Tom cried out in relief.

As Storm galloped up, Tom grabbed his mane and leapt into the saddle without breaking his stride. Elenna still ran alongside them. Tom reached down to pull her up behind him. They outpaced the villagers as they headed for the tunnels, Silver barking excitedly at the rear.

Outside the largest tunnel entrance, Tom tugged on the reins and brought Storm to a halt. He and Elenna slid to the ground.

"Well done, boy." Tom gave the black stallion a pat on the nose. "You came just in time!"

The sun was going down, the trees cast long shadows and the mouth of the tunnel looked darker than ever. Tom strode up to it. "I hope we're right, and this leads us to the Beast," he said.

"We really need those candles now," Elenna said, peering into the blackness.

Tom pulled a couple of them out

of his pocket. Elenna unfastened
the base of her quiver and took out
a flint. She struck a flame from
it with an arrowhead. The candle
flames burnt steadily, casting a circle
of yellow light as Tom and Elenna
stepped into the tunnel.

Tom heard the sound of pounding
footsteps outside, and glanced

back to see Raymond and the other
villagers appearing round a bend in
the path.

"Let's go – fast!" he urged Elenna.

With a candle in one hand, and
Storm's bridle in the other, Tom led
the way into the gloomy passage.
Elenna followed him, with Silver at
her heels. The wolf kept glancing

back and letting out threatening howls at the sound of the pursuing villagers. The noise filled the tunnel with echoes.

The candle flames dipped and wavered as Tom and the others hurried along, they cast moving shadows on the tunnel walls. Storm picked his way among the loose rocks on the tunnel floor, the clatter of his hooves sounding loud in the narrow passage.

Tom paused for a moment to listen. "I can't hear the villagers any more."

"Good." Elenna patted her wolf friend on the head. "I think Silver must have frightened them off."

Even though they were now safe from the evil villagers, Tom set a brisk pace as they carried on. There was no time to waste as long as Stealth prowled the streets of his beloved city.

"Which is the right way?" Elenna asked as they came to a place where the passage forked into two.

Tom hesitated, then chose the right-hand tunnel. "I think I remember the route from last time," he said.

He led the way up and down rocky slopes, through vast caves, and along passages with roofs so low that Storm could only just fit through. The candles burnt down, so Tom and Elenna had to stop and light two more.

Soon afterwards, they heard the sound of falling water ahead, and the candle flames lit up a stream that gushed out of the rock above them and fell into a pool below.

"I remember this," Elenna said. She set her candle down on a shelf in the rock so she could cup her hands under the stream and take a drink. "That's good. It's so cold!"

Tom drank too, and splashed his face, while Storm and Silver lapped from the pool.

As they continued, the tunnel started to slope upwards. Tom realised they were drawing close to the caves that opened in the hills just above The City. Excitement fluttered in his stomach. He drew his sword and held it at the ready, alert for any sign that Stealth was nearby.

Eventually Tom and Elenna climbed up a flight of shallow

stone steps.

"We're here!" Elenna exclaimed with a grin of satisfaction.

The steps led into another cave, Tom could see its jagged exit outlined against a starlit sky.

When he stepped onto the hillside he was about to blow out the candle, when he spotted markings on the ground in front of him. He squatted, holding the flame so its golden light poured down on them. Elenna came to peer over his shoulder.

"Pawprints," Tom whispered, a shiver of horror running through him. "Huge pawprints, just like in the village. Stealth must be waiting for us."

6

LOCKED OUT

Tom paused outside the city walls.
The gates stood open, and beyond
them the street was dark and quiet.

"Where are the guards?" Elenna
asked, her eyes wide as she gazed
around.

"I don't know." Tom felt his heart
thumping hard as he led the way
through the gates. "And where are
all the people?"

Even at this time of day, the city streets were usually full of market stalls, their lamps shining brightly on fruit and cheese or freshly baked bread and biscuits. The citizens would shop and gossip, while children darted to and fro among the stalls. But there were no lights, no sound of voices or laughter. All the doors and windows were tightly shut.

Storm's hooves sounded loud on the cobbles as Tom led him through the streets. Silver padded close to Elenna's side, his muzzle raised to sniff the air. The hairs on his neck were bristling as if he could sense an enemy, though there was nothing to be seen.

"It's like a ghost town," Elenna

whispered.

"Or a town ruled by a Ghost Beast," Tom added grimly.

As they turned a corner, Tom caught a glimpse of two flashes of bright yellow. Silver growled deep in his throat. Tom grabbed the hilt of his sword, but as he drew it the two yellow flashes darted away into the night.

Tom shivered. "I think we just spotted Stealth."

Elenna nodded, looking round apprehensively. "Where did he go?"

"I don't know. But we'd better keep our eyes open."

As Tom finished speaking, a threatening snarl curled through the air from behind him. Tom whipped round. How could the Beast have got there so quickly?

He glanced rapidly about them, his sword at the ready, but nothing moved in the darkness.

"This Beast is very good at hiding," Elenna remarked.

Tom nodded. "But Stealth is no coward," he said. "He'll show himself when he's ready."

The thought of a Ghost Beast stalking them made every hair on Tom's head prickle with tension, but he strode on determinedly towards the palace. "We've got to make sure King Hugo and Wizard Aduro are safe," he said.

At last, the street they were following led into the square in front of the palace. The gates to the palace grounds stood open, just like the gates to the city.

"There are no guards here, either," Elenna murmured.

They couldn't see any lights on in the palace as they passed through the gates, but as they approached the building, lamplight suddenly flickered through a window just above the main door. Tom looked up to see King Hugo gazing out. His face was ghostly pale.

"Greetings, Sire!" Tom called to him, relieved that the king was still alive.

King Hugo did not reply. He stared down at Tom and Elenna as if he were afraid of them.

Feeling even more uneasy, Tom tried to push open the palace door, but it was stuck fast. He rattled the handle, but the door still didn't move. It was locked!

"Please let us in, Sire," he called up to the king. "We've brought news."

For a moment King Hugo didn't reply. Tom exchanged a mystified glance with Elenna. He didn't understand this. He had never been denied entry to the palace before.

Another figure moved up beside King Hugo to look out of the window.

"Father!" Tom cried as he recognised Taladon.

Taladon didn't speak, either. After a moment, he shook his head sadly and moved away from the window again.

"Father, what's the matter?" Tom called. He felt as if the ground had just opened up beneath his feet. For his father to turn away from him like that, something must be really wrong. Tom thought he would burst with frustration if he didn't find out what it was.

Taladon didn't reappear, but King Hugo leant out of the window. "I'm sorry, Tom," he said. "We can't let you in. Stealth has been rampaging through The City. Every time he scratches someone, they turn to evil. No one can be trusted." For a moment the king hesitated, his face filled with grief. "I'm not even sure I can trust you and Elenna," he went on at last. "Pull up your sleeves, and let me see if you carry any panther claw-marks."

As Tom hesitated, he felt Elenna's hand on his arm. "King Hugo is right," she whispered. "We trusted the people of Stonewin, and remember how easily they tricked us! The king is doing the only thing he can – protecting the last sanctuary in Avantia. If evil got into the palace, then everything would be lost."

Tom let out a long breath. Elenna was right. If Avantia came to be ruled by an evil king, there would be no hope left. But it still hurt him to see mistrust in the eyes of the king he loved and served.

There was no point in pulling up his sleeves, he and Elenna could be carrying the marks of Stealth anywhere on their bodies.

"I understand, Sire," Tom replied. "Just tell me one thing – is Wizard Aduro safe?" His stomach lurched to think of Stealth scratching the

Good Wizard and turning him into another Malvel.

King Hugo nodded. "He is safe," he replied. "But his magic cannot undo the work of the Beast."

Tom bowed to the King and turned away. He paced through the gates again, followed by Elenna and their animal friends, and halted as another ghostly snarl swept across the empty square. Somewhere out there, a Beast was stalking the streets of The City. And Tom knew that it was his job to defeat it.

"While there's blood in my veins," he vowed, "I'll save Avantia!"

THE CLAWS OF STEALTH

Tom and Elenna crept through shifting light and darkness as clouds scudded across the face of the moon. The city streets were empty, but Tom knew that every corner, doorway or abandoned market stall could conceal Stealth.

He lugged aside a barrel full of rubbish to peer into the corner behind it, but he only disturbed a rat, which scuttled quickly away. On the other side of the street, Elenna was peering down a stairwell into the doorway of someone's cellar.

"Nothing here!" she called softly to Tom.

His sword at the ready, Tom led them further away from the palace. All the while, he was alert for the flash of amber eyes or the sound of evil snarling. But there was no sign of the Ghost Beast.

Suddenly Tom heard the sound of a door crashing open. Loud voices echoed in the still air, and the thud of footsteps came rapidly closer.

Elenna tugged at Tom's arm. "Quick – hide!"

Tom led Storm into the mouth of

a narrow alley. Elenna and Silver followed and pressed themselves against the wall. Peering out of the shadows, Tom saw a group of men and women burst into the street from around the nearest corner.

Their clothes were filthy and ragged. Tom could make out Stealth's claw-marks on some of them. All of them held weapons – knives, hammers and mallets. Their eyes seemed to glow with rage as they stumbled past the mouth of the alley. They banged on closed doors or pulled up cobbles from the street to throw at shuttered windows. Tom caught a glimpse of a man peering out from one of the houses, wide-eyed with terror, before slamming the shutters closed.

Tom felt sick as he watched them go. The citizens had been happy until the claws of Stealth had changed them. He tightened his grip on his sword, more determined than ever to find the ghostly panther and defeat it.

Elenna put a comforting hand on Tom's arm. "Maybe they'll be all right again," she suggested. "Just as soon as Stealth is dead."

They emerged from the alley and went on with their search, but the city was silent again and Stealth had not reappeared.

"This is hopeless," Tom said at last, halting beside a large inn on a street corner. "It will be dawn soon, and what will we do then? It could be dangerous to stay in the city in daylight."

"You mean it's not dangerous now?" Elenna's mouth twisted in a wry grin. "What's the matter with Silver?" she added. The wolf had raised his muzzle and was sniffing the air, his hackles rising. "Can you scent something, boy?"

Suddenly alert, Tom spun round.

At the same instant, a loud yowling split the silence. A huge black shape launched itself from the roof of the inn. Silver's warning had given Tom the seconds he needed to leap out of the way.

Stealth landed on the cobbles, panting lightly as the gaze from his yellow eyes locked with Tom's. His

gleaming white fangs were bared in a
snarl.

Tom heard an answering snarl
coming from Silver's throat. The
wolf's fur was bristling, his muscles
tensed to leap at the fierce panther.
Stealth towered over them, claws
unsheathed, ready to strike.

"Elenna, keep back," Tom warned.
"Don't let Silver or Storm come near."
What would happen if my friends

were turned to evil? he thought with horror.

"Silver!" Elenna's voice was commanding. "Silver, come here. You can't help."

The grey wolf let out a whine of protest, but he obeyed Elenna and followed her.

Tom was aware of his friend leading Storm and Silver further down the alley beside the inn, but he kept his gaze fixed on the Ghost Beast. He had never seen anything like it before.

Stealth's yellow eyes flared. His claws glittered. His huge ears swivelled back and forth, twitching at the slightest noise. But what turned the blood in Tom's veins to ice was the Beast's three tails, slashing through the air like whips.

Around the panther's neck was a thick leather collar, from which hung a scrap of gold. Tom's heart beat faster as he spotted it. The last piece of the Amulet of Avantia! If only he could get the fragment, his Quest would be complete. His father would no longer be a ghost.

Tom knew he couldn't risk coming within range of Stealth's claws or his three lashing tails. Raising his sword, he sent it whirling through the air in a shining arc. Stealth crouched to leap at Tom, but before he could take off, the spinning sword sliced through one of his tails, and fell clattering to the cobbles.

Blood as black as night spurted

from the wound, and Stealth let out a howl of rage and pain. Tom's eyes widened as the Beast shifted into his ghostly form: his body transformed to churning black smoke, outlined by shimmering scarlet light.

No! Tom thought. *Stealth is changing into his ghostly form to hide himself from me. How can I defeat a Beast I can't see?*

He darted forwards to retrieve his sword. Immediately, the panther changed back into flesh and blood, giving a terrifying snarl.

"You can't scare me, Stealth!" Tom called out bravely.

Stealth crouched on the cobbles, ready to spring at him. Tom was caught between the Beast and the wall of the inn. His sword lay out of reach, almost underneath the paws of the Beast.

An arrow whipped through the air from behind him, striking the panther between his yellow eyes. Stealth tossed his head with a snarl of fury, giving Tom the chance to grab his sword and scramble out of range.

"Thanks, Elenna!" he shouted, as another arrow struck the Beast on the shoulder.

Stealth bared his teeth menacingly. Tom could see how hungry he was for revenge. The huge Beast leapt into the air, his vast black shadow enveloping Tom. At the last second, Tom jumped aside.

But he didn't have his magical

leaping power anymore. As his feet hit
the uneven cobbles, he stumbled and
fell awkwardly, knocking the breath
out of his body.

Must move away, Tom thought, half-
stunned. *Must get up...*

But his body wouldn't obey him.
Unable to move, he watched with
horror as Stealth stretched out one paw,
his deadly claws bared, ready to attack.

ELENNA TO THE RESCUE

"No!" Elenna yelled.

Before the Beast's claws could score down Tom's arm, he saw his friend pull another arrow from her quiver. "Don't get too close!" he gasped.

Elenna loosed the arrow, it hit Stealth on the back of the neck and stuck there, quivering. The Ghost Beast snarled and twisted his head, his jaws snapping as he tried to grasp the shaft and pull it out.

Elenna ran forwards and grabbed Tom by the arm, hauling him to his feet and back out of range.

"Thanks!" Tom panted.

Shivers ran through his body as he realised what would have happened if his friend hadn't been so quick. He would have been turned to evil... Avantia's last hope would have gone.

"We need a different plan," he said to Elenna. "I can't risk getting near those claws."

Elenna nodded, but didn't reply. She was still watching the furious Beast, her bow raised and another arrow notched on the string.

Tom remembered how he had

swung himself through the air to escape from the store back in Stonewin. *That's it!* he told himself. *I need a rope!* If he could lasso Stealth and climb onto his back, the Ghost Beast wouldn't be able to reach him with his claws. *And then I can rescue the piece of the amulet from his collar,* Tom thought.

Glancing round, he saw a pile of barrels stacked up beside the wall of the inn, bound together by a piece of rope. Tom sheathed his sword and darted over to them, tugging desperately at the knotted coils.

Behind him, he heard a triumphant snarl, and glanced back to see that Stealth had finally wrenched the arrow out of his shoulder. His

gleaming teeth splintered the shaft and he tossed the scraps away.

I've got to get this rope loose now! Tom thought.

Stealth crouched again, snarling as he prepared to leap at Tom. At the same instant, the knot gave way and Tom pulled the rope free from the barrels.

He quickly twisted the rope to form a noose. As Stealth pounced, Tom ducked, and the huge panther leapt over him, whipping round as he landed to face Tom again.

Tom tossed the noose into the air and began to circle it. The Ghost Beast lashed out at him, but he was too big to manoeuvre himself properly in the narrow alley.

"Move back," Tom instructed Elenna. "We need more space. If we have to fight, we'll fight fair."

With his gaze fixed on the panther, he heard Elenna leading Storm away and the patter of Silver's paws on the cobbles. Tom followed them, walking backwards, circling the lasso over his head. Stealth stalked along the alley after him, his tails raking along the walls on either side.

As he emerged from the end of the alley, Tom realised that in their search for Stealth he and Elenna had traced a circle through The City. They had arrived back in the main square, not far from the palace gates.

Glancing up at the palace, Tom spotted the one lighted window, with

King Hugo, Wizard Aduro and his father, Taladon, all watching silently. *They've never seen anything like this,* Tom thought. *I only hope I come out the winner.*

Stealth had emerged from the alley too, and was prowling across the square towards Tom. Circling the lasso, Tom tried to judge the best moment to strike.

"Tom, be careful!" Elenna's voice had a warning note.

He realised that Stealth had understood what he was trying to do. The Beast was circling, one of his tails above his head, making a lasso of his own.

If he catches me, I'm done for, Tom told himself. *It's now or never!*

He had to lasso the Beast before
the Beast lassoed him first. And he
could see that Stealth's body was
gradually beginning to fade into its
ghostly form.

I've got to catch him before he changes! Tom realised. He sent the rope arcing through the air towards the panther. At the same time, Elenna fired a volley of arrows at the Beast's back legs. Stealth's head snapped round and he bared his teeth at her. The Beast had turned half-ghostly, but Tom could just make out enough of him to aim.

"Yes!" Tom's triumphant shout echoed across the square as the noose fell perfectly over the Ghost Beast's head.

Tom pulled the rope tight around Stealth's neck and ran to his side. Distracted by the struggle, it was clear that Stealth could no longer concentrate on becoming a ghost and

he returned to his full form. Gripping
the panther's collar in one hand, Tom
vaulted onto the Beast's back. Stealth
struggled to wrench the rope out of
Tom's hands, but Tom held it fast.

Stealth swung his head round, his
fangs snapping at Tom, but every
time he turned to get closer, Tom was
carried out of reach on the Beast's
own body. The rope burnt his hands
as he clung to it, trying to stay on the
ghost panther's twisting back.

Sitting astride the Beast, Tom drew
his sword again, gripping the rope
with his other hand. He managed
to scramble to his feet, but almost
lost his balance as Stealth reared
up on his hind legs in an effort to
shake Tom off. The panther's coal-

black fur was as slippery as ice. But Tom somehow clung to the rope and climbed up Stealth's spine until he was in reach of the collar.

With a single stroke, Tom sliced the collar through. It clattered to the ground, the piece of amulet ringing on the cobblestones of the square.

Stealth let out a final roar of pain and anger.

At the same instant, a fierce gust of wind blew through the square.

A whirling reddish-purple cloud began to form in front of Tom, and a scream of rage echoed through the air.

"Nooooooo!"

Tom recognised the voice. *Malvel!*

1

9

FIGHT AGAINST THE WIZARD

Tom scrambled down Stealth's leg to ground level. Stealth bared his teeth and began tugging at the rope to free himself. The reddish-purple cloud thickened, and Dark Wizard Malvel stepped out of it. His sunken eyes burned with rage. As his green cloak flapped like the wings of a hawk, he swooped down to grab the collar and the last piece of the amulet.

But Tom was too quick for him. He stepped forwards, kicking the collar out of his enemy's reach, and held his sword at Malvel's throat. The Dark Wizard staggered back, rage and fear in his eyes.

As Tom tried to follow him, Stealth slipped between them. His body was starting to turn ghostly again, though Tom could still see his faint outline.

Tom tried to dart between Stealth's ghostly legs to reach Malvel, but the panther moved to block him. Tom's outstretched arm passed through the Beast's smoky body. The icy touch made his arm numb, and he stumbled back, barely able to keep hold of his sword.

Recovering quickly, Tom made another dash for Malvel, but once again Stealth got in his way. *This Beast is too clever!* Tom thought angrily.

Malvel raised his hands, ready to cast a spell. Tom shivered as Malvel began to chant in a thunderous voice. Tom knew he had no protection against magic!

He braced himself for a desperate leap at the Dark Wizard. But then he heard Elenna's voice. "Tom! Here – catch!"

His friend had grabbed Stealth's collar from the ground. She tossed it to Tom, who caught it in his free hand. Triumph flooded through him.

He had all the pieces of the Amulet of Avantia!

As soon as Tom's fingers closed round the collar, dazzling light poured out of the scrap of gold, forming a protective orb around him. Purple fire streamed from Malvel's fingers, but when it hit the orb it ricocheted off harmlessly and disappeared.

Malvel let out a shriek of rage as his spell failed. Tom lunged forwards. "Avantia!" he cried, slicing his sword through the air. Malvel leapt away, but the tip of Tom's sword scored through his flesh, opening a gash in his cheek.

The Dark Wizard screamed with pain and fury. "You'll regret

that, boy!"

Before Tom could strike him again, he stepped back into the cloud, which exploded in a burst of purple light. Tom had to shield his eyes against it. The silver orb that had protected Tom died away too.

Stealth's ghostly form whipped round to attack him. Gripping his sword, Tom braced himself, ready to fight. But as the smoky outline of the Beast began to fade, Tom heard the last echo of a snarl as Stealth vanished completely.

Tom stood panting, gazing at the spot where the Ghost Beast had disappeared. "He's gone," he said in a hoarse voice. "Stealth has gone for good."

Elenna hurried to his side, with Storm and Silver close behind her. "Tom, that was great!"

"I wouldn't have survived if you hadn't thrown me the piece of amulet," Tom replied. "And I only managed to wound Malvel. That slash on his cheek won't kill him."

"You're right, boy." Malvel's voice spoke from the emptiness. He spat a curse at Tom. "Our fight is far from over. I'll be back!"

"Good!" Tom called out in reply. "I'll look forward to it." Remembering the look of fury and frustration on the Dark Wizard's face as blood poured from his cheek, Tom felt courage surge through him. Malvel could be wounded – he could be killed! If he ever had to face the Dark Wizard again, Tom had some extra knowledge about his enemy now. But he could think about that another day. Turning to Elenna, he said, "We've finished our Quest! And now I can meet my father properly."

10

HOME TO ERRINEL?

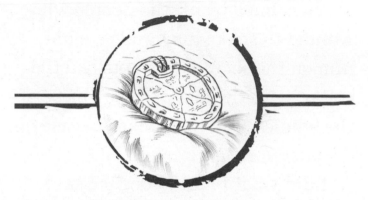

Shouting broke out behind Tom. He spun round, his sword at the ready, braced for another attack.

The citizens of Avantia were flinging open the doors and windows of the houses around the square. They streamed out into the streets, laughing and shouting joyfully as they surrounded Tom and Elenna.

"We're free!"

"Well done! You killed the Beast!"

Tom sheathed his sword, almost overwhelmed by all the people who wanted to shake his hand or clap him on the shoulder. He pushed the collar, with the last precious piece of the amulet, into his pocket in case he dropped it in the crowd.

"I did what I had to do," he said. "And I couldn't have done it without Elenna."

Elenna grinned.

Then the people grew quieter, and moved back. Tom saw that the palace door had opened, and King Hugo was striding across the square towards him. Tom began to kneel as his king approached, but King Hugo grasped him by the shoulders and drew him into an embrace.

"You've saved Avantia!" he exclaimed. Releasing Tom, he added, "I'm sorry for locking you out of the palace. The risk was just too great."

"I understand," Tom replied. "You were only trying to protect the kingdom."

With an arm round his shoulders, King Hugo led Tom back towards the palace. Elenna followed, leading Storm, with Silver bounding alongside.

A golden light was growing beyond the palace roof, showing where the sun would rise. Malvel's evil had vanished along with the night.

Inside the palace courtyard, a servant led Storm away to be

groomed and fed, while King Hugo took Tom and Elenna inside. Silver padded quietly along behind.

The king led Tom and Elenna down the stairs and along a stone passage to a heavy door studded with brass nails.

"This is the armour room," Tom realised.

"That's right," said King Hugo. "And the very end of your Quest will happen here."

Tom followed him into the room. It was familiar to him from the start of his second Beast Quest, when he recovered the Golden Armour. He remembered the rough stone walls and the torches in metal holders, and the wooden stand for the armour that stood in the middle of the room.

King Hugo's master of arms stood beside the wooden stand. He smiled as he saw Tom and Elenna. "Welcome back," he said. His pet ferret poked its head out of his pocket and added a friendly squeak.

Silver let out a questioning whine as he spotted the little creature, and Elenna rested a hand on his neck.

"It's all right, boy," she murmured. "He's a friend."

Wizard Aduro stepped forwards. "Well done, Tom," he said. "Your courage has saved Avantia once again."

Embarrassed, Tom exchanged a glance with Elenna. "We did it together."

"And now you must finish your Quest," Aduro went on. "Come."

He gestured for Tom to approach a small table that stood beside the wall. A crimson velvet cushion lay upon it. "This is the rightful resting place of the Amulet of Avantia," the wizard said.

Tom took the leather thong from around his neck and laid the amulet carefully on the velvet cushion. Then he pulled Stealth's collar out of his pocket and unfastened the final scrap of gold. He fitted it carefully into the gap that waited for it.

Golden light flared up, filling the room and dazzling Tom's eyes. He heard Elenna gasp in surprise.

When the light faded, Tom saw that

the Amulet of Avantia was complete once more. He drew a long breath of satisfaction. *That's what King Hugo meant. Now my Beast Quest is really over.*

"Tom, look!" Elenna exclaimed.

Tom turned to see that the suit of Golden Armour had reappeared

on the wooden stand. The master
at arms had already taken out a
handkerchief and was polishing the
gleaming breastplate.

Then a man stepped out from
behind the Golden Armour. Tom
caught his breath as he recognised
his father, Taladon. But he had never
seen Taladon looking like this. He
seemed taller and broader than ever,
his eyes shone and the pink of good
health glowed in his cheeks.

He put his arms round Tom in a
tight embrace. This time Tom could
feel his warmth and strength. It was
how he had always dreamt of meeting
his father.

"Congratulations, Tom," Taladon
said, stepping back. "And you too,

Elenna. I'm proud of you both. I knew you wouldn't fail."

"The whole of Avantia owes them thanks," Wizard Aduro said.

King Hugo led the way out of the armour room and back up the stairs to his throne room. The balcony windows stood open, and Tom could hear the sound of the crowd outside in the square.

"Come, Taladon," King Hugo said. "I must announce your return."

The noise outside swelled to a welcoming roar as King Hugo and Taladon stepped out onto the balcony.

Tom and Elenna followed them with Silver close beside Elenna.

Morning sunlight lit up the square

and the crowds of people, who were
still streaming in from all directions.
King Hugo raised his hands for
silence, but it was a while before he
could make himself heard.

"Good citizens of Avantia," he
began. "I bring you wonderful news.
The kingdom's greatest hero, Taladon

the Swift, has finally returned."

Taladon stepped forwards to take a bow and the crowd went wild, waving and cheering and tossing their hats into the air.

"Now that Taladon is here, what are you going to do?" Elenna asked Tom, as his father waved to the crowd.

Tom heard footsteps behind him and looked round to see that Wizard Aduro was watching them closely, a gentle smile on his face. "Are you glad your journey is over?" he asked. "Do you want to go home to Errinel?"

Tom opened his mouth to reply, and stopped. He had often felt homesick for his village, and longed to see his aunt and uncle again, but he found it hard to imagine settling back into life at the forge.

Something in Aduro's voice, or the gleam in his eyes, sent a prickle of knowledge creeping up Tom's spine. "I'm not going back to Errinel, am I?"

Aduro shook his head. As the cheers of the crowd echoed in their ears, he drew Tom and Elenna back into the shadows of the throne room.

"You will have some time to spend with your father," the Good Wizard promised. "But after that, you may be needed elsewhere." His finger curled, beckoning. "Follow me. I have something to show you... The most difficult Quests are yet ahead."

Tom exchanged a glance with Elenna. He didn't know what Wizard Aduro meant, but he realised that his path was leading him to new dangers. His breath came faster, and he shivered with a mixture of fear and excitement.

Am I ready? he asked himself.

Beside him, Elenna's eyes were shining, and Silver had cocked his head alertly, as if he wanted to set out right away.

Yes! Tom straightened his shoulders as triumph flooded through him. *While there's blood in my veins, I'll serve Avantia!*

CONGRATULATIONS, YOU HAVE COMPLETED THIS QUEST!

At the end of each chapter you were awarded a special gold coin. The QUEST in this book was worth an amazing 11 coins.

Look at the Beast Quest totem picture inside the back cover of this book to see how far you've come in your journey to become

MASTER OF THE BEASTS.

The more books you read, the more coins you will collect!

Do you want your own
Beast Quest Totem?

1. Cut out and collect the coin below
2. Go to the Beast Quest website
3. Download and print out your totem
4. Add your coin to the totem
www.beastquest.co.uk/totem

Don't miss the first exciting book in this series, NIXA THE DEATH BRINGER!

Read on for a sneak peek...

CHAPTER ONE

A FATHER RETURNS

"One hundred and fifty-one! One hundred and fifty-two!" Captain Harkman's voice echoed across the training courtyard.

Tom groaned as he pumped his

arms in yet another press-up. He thought he was going to die of boredom, if he didn't first melt into a puddle under the hot sun of Avantia.

He remembered how he had returned from Gorgonia a few weeks before, fresh from the Quest where he had defeated the Dark Wizard, Malvel, for the third time.

"Avantia owes you a great debt," King Hugo had said. "Tom, you may choose any position you like in my court. Ask, and it's yours."

"Thank you, sire," Tom had replied. "I'd like to be a soldier in your army."

He'd thought it would be fun, and a great way to go on helping Avantia. "But I was wrong." He sighed to himself. What was the point of doing press-ups all day long when he had powers that the cadet officer, Captain Harkman, had never dreamt of?

"I made a mistake," Tom muttered to himself as his arms pumped up and down. "I wish there was something else I could do.

Maybe another Quest…"

He snatched a glance across the courtyard to where his friend, Elenna, was teaching archery to the youngest cadets. He watched her positioning one boy's fingers on the bowstring, and saw his face break into a delighted grin as his arrow thumped home.

Tom heard heavy footsteps. Captain Harkman's feet halted beside him; he was tapping his whip against his polished riding boots.

"Slacking again?" Captain Harkman snarled. He crouched down beside Tom, so that Tom could see his red, sweating face and gingery hair. "You're just like your father. He was a slacker, too."

Fury flooded through Tom. He gritted his teeth together with the effort of controlling his temper.

"Taladon trained here once, when he was a young man," the Captain went on, straightening up. "He had all the skill in Avantia, but he was also cocky. The cockiest cadet I ever—"

Tom heard the sound of an arrow whizzing through the air. It just missed Captain Harkman's head as he ducked and rolled away.

"Who fired that?" he yelled, bouncing to his feet again.

Elenna ran over, bow in hand, and halted in front of the Captain.

"Sorry," she said. "It was one of my cadets. He hasn't quite got the hang of archery yet."

Tom hid a smile. He knew perfectly well that Elenna had fired the arrow herself. Just because they weren't on a Beast Quest didn't mean that he and Elenna wouldn't watch each other's backs anymore.

A voice called out from the palace gardens. "He has returned! Taladon the Swift has returned!"

Tom froze. Taladon? My father?

Breathlessly, he scrambled to his feet and pounded towards the archway that separated the training courtyard from the gardens, weaving his way between his fellow cadets.

"Hey! You there! Come back!"

Tom ignored Captain Harkman's shouts. He didn't care how the

Captain would punish him, if only he could see his father.

He heard light footsteps racing behind. He knew who that would be – Elenna.

Bursting through the archway, Tom saw one of the king's messengers dashing across the gardens. "He's here!" he yelled. "Taladon has returned!"

Tom took the steps up to the main palace door three at a time. The guards by the open doors waved him through and he ran down the long corridor that led towards King Hugo's throne room.

My father left when I was a baby, he thought. Am I really going to see him now?

Dashing around a corner, Tom came to a halt. The throne-room doors were open and a man was stepping through them. The sun slanting through a nearby window outlined his broad shoulders and long, black cloak. He strode forwards confidently, his head held high.

"Father!" Tom sprang towards him, but the man didn't seem to have heard. He walked on without looking back, and the guards pulled the throne-room doors closed behind him.

"Father?" Tom repeated to himself, as he stood alone in the corridor.

Read

NIXA THE DEATH BRINGER
to find out more!

FIGHT THE BEASTS,
FEAR THE MAGIC

Are you a BEAST QUEST mega fan?
Do you want to know about all the latest news,
competitions and books before anyone else?

Then join our Quest Club!

Visit the BEAST QUEST website
and sign up today!

www.beastquest.co.uk

Discover the new Beast Quest mobile game from

Available free on iOS and Android

Guide Tom on his Quest to free the Good Beasts
of Avantia from Malvel's evil spells.

Battle the Beasts, defeat the minions,
unearth the secrets and collect
rewards as you journey through the
Kingdom of Avantia.

DOWNLOAD THE APP TO BEGIN
THE ADVENTURE NOW!

WELCOME TO

Collect the special coins in this book. You will earn one gold coin for every chapter you read.

Once you have finished all the chapters, find out what to do with your gold coins at the back of the book.

With special thanks to Cherith Baldry

For Adam Dawkins

www.beastquest.co.uk

ORCHARD BOOKS

First published in Great Britain in 2009 by The Watts Publishing Group
This edition published in 2015

5 7 9 10 8 6 4

Text © 2009 Beast Quest Limited.
Cover and inside illustrations by Steve Sims
© Beast Quest Limited 2009

Beast Quest is a registered trademark of Beast Quest Limited
Series created by Beast Quest Limited, London

A CIP catalogue record for this book is available from the British Library.

ISBN 978 1 40834 821 5

Printed and bound in Great Britain by Clays Ltd, Elcograf S.p.A.

MIX
Paper from
responsible sources
FSC
www.fsc.org   FSC® C104740

The paper and board used in this book are made from wood from responsible sources

Orchard Books
An imprint of Hachette Children's Group
Part of The Watts Publishing Group Limited
Carmelite House, 50 Victoria Embankment, London EC4Y 0DZ

An Hachette UK Company
www.hachette.co.uk
www.hachettechildrens.co.uk